Squeaky Cleaners

in a hole!

Vivian French
illustrated by
Anna Currey

Hodder
Children's
Books

a division of Hodder Headline plc

To my nieces
Anna Currey

Text copyright © Vivian French 1996
Illustrations copyright © Anna Currey 1996

The right of Vivian French and Anna Currey to be identified
as the Author and the Illustrator of the Work has been asserted by them
in accordance with the Copyright, Designs and Patents Act 1988.

10   9   8   7   6   5   4   3   2

ISBN 0340 640677

Printed and bound in Great Britain by
Cox & Wyman Ltd, Reading, Berks

Hodder Children's Books
a Division of Hodder Headline plc
338 Euston Road
London NW1 3BH

One

It was very late at night. Fred was fast asleep in bed and snoring gently, but Nina and Gina were tiptoeing round the kitchen.

'I've hidden the biscuits and buns in the cupboard,' Gina whispered.

Nina nodded. 'Good! Do you want to help me ice the cake?'

Gina shook her head. 'You do it. I'll make some cheese sandwiches. Then it'll all be ready! Birthday breakfast!'

Nina chuckled. 'Won't he be surprised?' And she carefully wrote HAPPY BIRTHDAY, FRED in blue icing on the top of the cake.

Gina yawned, and peered at Nina.
'What are you writing now?'

'SUPER MOUSE,' Nina said. 'Oh
bother! The icing's gone all runny!'
Gina patted Nina's arm. 'I'm sure
he'll like it, dear,' she said, and yawned
again. 'Eeek! I'm tired!'

As Nina and Gina curled up and closed their eyes, Fred sat up.

For some time his nose had been twitching, and now he was wide awake. He hopped out of bed and went to investigate.

The kitchen was very warm. Fred
sniffed again. 'Cake!' he said to himself.
'Tee Hee! It must be my birthday cake!'

He opened
the larder
door. 'Hmm,'
he thought.
'Maybe I
should have
a little peep,
just to see
what sort of
cake it is . . .'

Two

TAP TAP TAP . . . TAP TAP TAP . . .

The three Squeaky Cleaners woke up
with a start.

'Go away!' grumbled Fred. He
brushed a few tickly cake crumbs off his
whiskers and shut his eyes firmly.

'Who's that?' called Nina.

'Burglars!' gasped Gina.

'Really, Gina! Burglars don't knock,'
Nina said, putting on her dressing-gown.
She hurried to the front door.

Outside was a large and anxious mole.

'Er . . . are you the Squeaky Cleaners?' he asked.

'Only during the daytime,' Nina said crossly. 'At this time of night we're the sleepy cleaners.'

The mole burst into tears.

Nina sighed heavily, and shook her head. 'You'd better come in,' she said.

It took two boxes of paper hankies
before anyone could understand a word
the mole was saying. He quivered and
sobbed, but eventually Nina nodded.

'I see,' she said. 'You're having a
party, and you've invited all your
friends, but your home is in a mess?'

The mole snuffled into the last of the paper hankies.

'Yes . . . it's all dreadful!'

Nina patted him on the back. 'Don't worry. We'll help. When's your party?'

The mole threw a hankie over his head. 'TONIGHT!' he wailed. 'That's why I had to come and see you now! Everyone's arriving at six o'clock this evening!'

Nina, Gina and Fred looked at each other. Fred groaned loudly.

Nina glanced at the clock. It was six o'clock in the morning.

'Right!' said Nina. 'Everybody UP and OUT!'

Three

The mole was right about his home
being a mess. Even Gina turned pale
when she saw the heaps of rubble and
mud and the messy footprints
everywhere.

'Gina and I will unload the van,'
Nina said. 'Fred–' she stopped, and
looked round.

Fred was leaning
against his motorbike,
fast asleep.

'FRED!' Nina shouted. 'Wake up!'

'Eh? What? Oh, I wasn't asleep,' Fred said.

Nina snorted. 'Hurry up and bring in the buckets and mops.'

Soap suds and bubbles floated up to the ceiling of the mole's home as the Squeaky Cleaners began to clean. Nina rubbed and scrubbed. Fred swept the dirt out of the mole's front door. Gina polished the woodwork.

'Goodness!'
said the mole
admiringly.
'What a shine!'

Gina shooed him away. 'Excuse me,
Mr Mole,' she said. 'Why don't you get
the party food ready?'

'Food?' said the mole. 'Oh, yes! It's all in my larder. I'll go and see if it's all right.' He trundled happily off down a side tunnel.

It was Gina who saw the first worm.
It came wriggling up from the side
tunnel. Gina let out a loud squeak and
snatched at a broom.

'SHOO!' she shrieked. 'You horrid
slimy thing!'

The worm put on a frantic
turn of speed and shot
off towards
the front
door.

There was a puffing and a panting,
and the mole came chasing up.
'Did you – *puff* –
see my – *puff* –
worm?'

Gina stared at him.

'Your worm?'

The mole nodded. 'It got away when I opened the larder door!'

'Eeeek!' Nina waved her paw at the side tunnel. 'Look! Look!'

Gina, Fred and the mole swung round.

A motley collection of beetles, slugs, snails and worms were tiptoeing out.

When they saw Nina, Gina, Fred and the mole they ran, slithered and slid in all directions.

'My party food!' shouted the mole. 'STOP! STOP! Come back!'

There was wild confusion. Several beetles scuttled up the walls, the worms tied themselves in knots, and a large slug did its best to trip the mole up.

Gina screamed and ran away. Nina waved her brush fiercely.

Fred leant against the wall and laughed.

The mole sat down and burst into
tears. Nina put down her broom and
tut-tutted loudly.

'You must stop crying whenever
anything goes wrong,' she said.

'But it's not just anything,' the mole
howled. 'It's *all* gone wrong! I was going
to have a lovely party but now my party
food is running away and it's made my
house all messy again!'

Fred stopped laughing. He and Nina stared.

All the shiny clean tunnels were covered in muddy worm tracks, snail slime and beetle prints.

Gina came
back, peering
cautiously
all around
her.

'Have all those horrid slugs and
snails gone?' she asked anxiously.
Nina nodded.

'Good,' Gina said. 'Then we'd better get . . .' her voice died away as she saw the mess. 'Oh!'

'Exactly,' Nina said. 'I think we'd better have a plan. Mole, blow your nose!'

Four

It was Nina's plan. Gina was far too
worried about the possibility of worms
popping round the corner to pay much
attention. Fred sat down and dozed. The
mole snuffled quietly.

'Fred,' Nina said, 'you and Mole must make sure there are no worms or beetles hiding in the tunnels. If there are, take them back to Mole's larder. Then you can stay and guard them – we can't have any more escapes!'

Gina shuddered.
'Oh, dear me, no!'

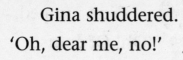

Mole nodded.
Fred didn't
answer.

'FRED!' snapped
Nina. Fred opened
one eye.
'And Gina,'
Nina went on, 'I'm
afraid you and I will
be cleaning up this
mess.'

Gina jumped.
'Oh! Of course,
dear,' she said,
and picked up
a scrubbing
brush.

Nina sighed as she went to fill up
her bucket. 'Here we go again!' she said.

Fred followed Mole down the winding passages. There were no beetles, worms or slugs – only a great number of worm wriggles and beetle prints.

They finally reached Mole's larder which wasn't so much a larder as a large room. When Mole opened the door Fred took a step back. He was expecting to be knocked over by another rush of escaping dinners.

Nothing happened.

'Oh, no!' said Mole. 'All my dinners have escaped!' His voice wobbled. 'There isn't even one slug or worm left!'

Fred scratched his head as he looked round. It was true. Every shelf and cupboard was empty.

'Well,' he said, 'I can't say I care for worms myself. But if it's what you and your friends like . . . '

His eye was caught by a small bag in a corner. 'What's that? Is it food?'

The mole looked puzzled. 'I don't know.' He went over to the bag. 'Oh! Oh! Oh!'

Fred followed him and looked over his shoulder. The bag was full of letters.

COME TO MY PARTY 6 O'CLOCK LOTS OF FOOD! LOVE MOLE

'Ah!' said Fred thoughtfully. 'You forgot to send the invitations!'

'BOOOOOOOHOOOOOOOOOOOOOOOOO
BOOOOOOOOOO
HOOOOOOO
BOOOOO
HOO!'

The mole turned into a miserable,
squashy howling heap.

'I WANTED A PAAAAAAAARTY!' he
bawled. 'A PAAAAAAAARTY!'

Something clicked in Fred's head.
A party!
BIRTHDAYS!
His birthday!

It was today – and he and Nina and
Gina had been so busy with this
miserable mole that they had all
forgotten!

Of course!
Fred let out
a loud squeak
and ran.

He ran
down the
Mole's tunnels,
past Nina
and Gina.

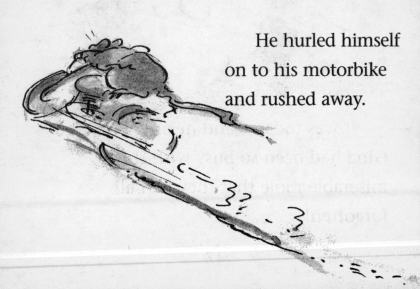

He hurled himself
on to his motorbike
and rushed away.

Nina and Gina stared at each other.
'Whatever's happening?' Nina asked.
Gina shook her head.

Nina sighed. 'We'd better go and see
to that mole,' she said.
'He's crying –
again.'

The mole eventually stopped
weeping and wailing.

'I'm so sorry,' he whimpered. 'I've made it a horrible day for you. I wouldn't have made such a fuss . . . but I've never, ever had a birthday party and I did so want just one.'

'Goodness!' said Nina. 'So it's your birthday! You didn't say! Happy birthday!'

The mole sniffed. 'But it isn't, is it?' he said sorrowfully. 'It's a very unhappy birthday!'

'Eeeek!' said Gina. 'It's Fred's birthday too! I'd quite forgotten!'

'Hmm,' Nina said. 'I wonder just what Fred is up to?'

Five

There was a scuffling sound in the
distance. A light shone from round the
corner; a flickering glow that lit up all
the passageway.

Gina and Nina and the mole sat up.
Fred appeared carrying a huge tray,
heaped with cheese sandwiches, buns
and biscuits. In the centre was half a
cake, lit with candles. As he carried it
closer the mole clapped his paws.

'Look! Oh, look! It says "SUPER
MOLE"! Oh, however did you do it? Oh,
this is the best birthday I've ever had!'

Nina and Gina looked at the cake.
The half that was left did indeed say
'SUPER MO' and then a squiggle.

Fred nodded. 'Super mole,' he said.
'That's it.' He winked at Nina and Gina.

Six

The Squeaky Cleaners reached home
and collapsed.

'Phew!' said Fred. 'All I want to do is
go to bed!'

'I'm sorry, Fred,' Nina said. 'It wasn't
much of a birthday.'

Gina turned to Nina.

'But Fred was so clever – didn't you

notice? He only brought half the cake!
The half that says "HAPPY BIRTHDAY,
FRED" is still here. We could have a
little celebration now!'

'Good idea!' said Nina. 'Where did you put it, Fred?'

Fred coughed. 'Um . . . actually, I think I'm much too full to eat anything else. I think I'll just go to bed now . . .' And he pottered away.

Nina and Gina looked at each other
in surprise.

'Odd,'
said Nina.
She got up,
and went
to look in
the larder.

She came back grinning.

'Ha!' she said. 'I've got a feeling Fred did have his birthday breakfast after all. He just had it all by himself – in the middle of the night!'

'I didn't see any crumbs,' Gina said
doubtfully.

'Of course you didn't,' Nina said, and laughed. 'He may be greedy, but he's a Squeaky Cleaner – and the Squeaky Cleaners are the best!'